Rosie and the Rustlers

ROY GERRARD

A SUNBURST BOOK • FARRAR, STRAUS AND GIROUX

Where the mountains meet the prairie, where the men are wild and hairy,
    There's a little ranch where Rosie Jones is boss.
It's a place that's neat and cozy, and the boys employed by Rosie
    Work extremely hard, to stop her getting cross.

Next to Rose is Fancy Dan, on his left is Salad Sam,
    One-Leg Smith and Singing Sid and Mad McGhee.
And then there's Utah Jim, who looks nice but rather dim —
    Quite a decent bunch of boys they seem to me.

In the saddle every day, well, they sure do earn their pay
  Doing wrangling and lassoing and such stuff.
When it's windy or it's raining, you won't hear the boys complaining,
  For the life they lead makes cowboys pretty tough.

When their hard day's work is done and it's time to have some fun
   They all gather in the bunkhouse for the night.
Sam whips up some lovely salads, Sidney sings them charming ballads,
   And they serenade till turning out the light.

On the day they went to see their dear friends the Cherokee
    They left Mad McGhee behind to guard the cattle.
Though they went without a care, there was trouble in the air,
    Which involved McGhee in something of a battle.

For the outlaw Greasy Ben and his ruffianly men
   Soon came galloping along to Rosie's place.
They were sinister and seedy, good-for-nothing, grim and greedy,
   And their manners were a positive disgrace.

The moment they detected that the ranch was ill protected
They took out their guns and shot at Mad McGhee.
And although their bullets missed, he was powerless to resist,
So he did the prudent thing, which was to flee.

There were scenes of consternation and of outraged indignation
When they heard McGhee describe what had occurred.
Then they galloped home at speed, so that Ben should not succeed
In escaping to the mountains with their herd.

They arrived home just in time to prevent the wicked crime,
And the frightened outlaws fled across the plain.
They had saved the herd, it's true, and yet Rosie really knew
That the gang would try to steal their steers again.

Hawkeye John, the Indian chief, said he'd help them track the thief
    And his braves would guard the ranch while they were gone.
So they set off there and then, on the trail of Greasy Ben,
    And their hazardous adventure was begun.

They pursued them night and day to the mountains far away
    As they followed tracks that John alone could see,
Till at last they thought it best to pitch camp and have a rest,
    So they stopped and ate a buffalo for tea.

Having spent a restful night, they all woke up feeling bright,
  Though the ground was hard and lumpy, to be sure.
They put on their hats and jeans, had some coffee and some beans,
  Then they mounted up and hit the trail once more.

It's a blessing they were tough, for the trail became quite rough,
  Which occasioned them to quit their horses' backs,
But they struggled bravely on, very glad of Hawkeye John,
  Who, amazingly, could still discern the tracks.

With great doggedness and care they searched out the bandits' lair,
  Till they found the shack of Ben and all his crew,
And then Rosie and her boys, being sure to make no noise,
  Found a hiding place, then wondered what to do.

Until up spoke Utah Jim (you will all remember him —
     He's the one his friends considered none too bright),
And they seemed inclined to sneer, till they heard his neat idea
     For ensnaring Greasy Ben without a fight.

He declared he'd bet his shirt one or other would get hurt
     If they used the normal method of attack.
What they really ought to do was to take up a lasso
     And then throw it round the chimney of the shack.

Next they'd all tug on the rope, in the optimistic hope
    That they'd pull the outlaws' shack into the pool.
The boys thought this fantastic and waxed enthusiastic,
    For they saw that Utah Jim was no one's fool.

So then Rosie kissed his cheek and declared he was unique —
    His complexion turned a lively shade of pink.
To complete his satisfaction, when his plan went into action,
    They fared better than he'd even dared to think.

The log cabin gave a lurch, then it toppled from its perch
   And it landed with a satisfying splosh.
When the bandits crawled ashore, they were shocked and wet and sore,
   But much cleaner from their unexpected wash.

Rosie Jones was quite enraptured, now the wicked gang was captured
(Though she felt relieved that none had chanced to drown).
So once more they hit the trail, to put Ben and Co. in jail,
And the folks all cheered when Rosie came to town.

Then the sheriff was well pleased that the bandits had been seized,
 And the townsfolk gathered round them to applaud.
Rosie's gallant little band became famed throughout the land,
 And they got five hundred dollars as reward.

Rosie held a celebration for the local population
To express her thanks for what her friends had done.
There was dancing in the street, and delicious things to eat,
So that everybody had enormous fun.

Where the mountains meet the prairie, where the men are wild and hairy,
    There's a little ranch where Rosie reigns supreme.
Where the grass could not be greener, where the air could not be cleaner,
    Life is happy, life is peaceful — it's a dream.